THE MUM TRAP

Andersen Young Readers' Library

THE MUM TRAP

RUTH SYMES

Andersen Press · London

With love to Sylvia – my Mum

First published in 2000 by
Andersen Press Limited,
20 Vauxhall Bridge Road, London SW1V 2SA
Reprinted 2000, 2004

British Library Cataloguing in Publication Data available
ISBN 0 86264 933 1

Typeset by FSH, London WC1
Printed and bound in Great Britain by Bookmarque, Croydon, Surrey

Chapter 1

The mum trap wasn't something Gem and I planned exactly. It just sort of happened. I suppose you could blame it on the 'Polly's People' show. That's where we got the idea from.

'Polly's People' is a talk show – a bit like Oprah. Me and my sister always watch it. Dad's usually too busy, making the dinner.

Anyway, one week Polly did this show about lonely heart adverts. She interviewed lots of people who'd met each other by advertising in the personal columns.

'He could be our dad, Anna,' Gem said, as we sat together on the sofa and watched one man, a widower like Dad, tell how he'd put an advert in his local paper and got more replies from interested ladies than he knew what to do with.

We both had the idea at the same time.

'Dad's birthday present!'

We wanted to get him something special, but hadn't been sure what. Now we knew. We'd find Dad a new wife – and a new mum for us.

'Dinner's nearly ready!' Dad called from the kitchen. The smell of chips wafted into the living room.

'Okay,' we called back.

I stood up and unplugged Gem's electric wheelchair from the socket. The battery needs to be charged up overnight if it's to keep running the next day. I pressed the on button and a green light lit up. I used the steering joystick on one of the chair arms to direct it over to Gem.

'Thanks,' she said, pressing the stop button. She swung herself in and clicked the safety strap shut.

Luckily Dad had been too busy cooking to see any of the programme. So he didn't know what we were thinking of doing.

I was sure he'd be pleased, once he started getting replies to his advert, especially if one of them was from someone very nice. But I was equally sure if we suggested advertising him in the local paper he'd say, 'No way.'

So we had to do it for him.

'Good "Polly's People" show?' Dad asked, over the fish fingers and chips.

'Yeah, great,' we told him.

After dinner Gem and I cleaned up the kitchen. I washed and Gem dried as usual.

'Look at this!' I said.

Dad had peeled the potatoes, for the chips, on the lonely hearts page of our local paper – the *Medlock Times*.

'Let's see,' Gem said.

I brushed the peelings into the bin and we read through the potato-stained adverts.

'You two okay out there?' Dad called from the living room.

'Yes,' we called back.

'I'm going to take a shower.'

'Okay.'

We carried on reading.

Gem pointed to an advert. '"Ugly, forty-year-old, twice broken-hearted man seeks lady for fun and romance,"' she whispered.

'At least he's honest,' I said. 'I expect most of them aren't.'

'This one sounds like Mr Jenkins, the music teacher at my school,' Gem said, pointing to another advert. '"Opera-loving musical man (36) seeks petite lady."'

'I've just had a nasty thought,' I said.

'What?'

'What if someone we know replies to Dad's advert – Medlock's only a small town. What if one of our teachers gets in touch?'

'I wouldn't mind if someone from my school did,' Gem said, 'unless it was Miss Bannister – she's horrible!'

'I suppose it'd be all right,' I said. But I hoped none of the teachers at my school replied to the advert. I'd die of embarrassment if Dad went on a date with one of them. What if someone in my class found out? And what if Dad and the teacher got romantic? And he *kissed* her. Just the thought of it made me feel a bit sick.

'Hey, this one looks like she'd suit my music teacher,' Gem said. '"Lady pianist (40) wltm musical ear attached to an attractive man." What's wltm mean?'

'Would like to meet.'

I looked at the other adverts.

'I like this,' I said. '"Toad (50) seeks Princess to help him turn into a Prince."'

Gem laughed. 'That's a good one.'

'There's another one a bit like it,' I said and read aloud, '"Maid Marion (38) wltm an honest Robin for long walks in the forest."'

'How about putting "Three bears wltm Goldilocks" for our advert?' Gem said.

I laughed, 'Or, "Three little pigs wltm a builder"?'

'Or, "Handsome hero with two angelic daughters wltm Princess Charming,"' Gem said, flicking back her hair.

'Uurgh! Sickly.'

'We'll need to put in Dad's age,' Gem said, 'all the other advertisers have.'

'How about "Handsome and Fun Widower, 40, with two daughters, aged 13 and 10, wltm someone special"?' I said.

'Okay.'

I found a pen and filled in the boxes for people who wanted to advertise, at the bottom of the page.

'How much does it cost?' Gem asked.

'A tenner.'

We each put in half the money.

'Right,' I said when the envelope was addressed, stamped and ready to be posted. 'You absolutely sure this is a good idea for Dad's birthday?'

'Yes!' said Gem. 'Good for him and good for us too. I want a new mum.'

I nodded. It was time. Dad needed someone else in his life and so did we.

My ideal new mum would be someone who could French plait my hair, like Jenny Carter's, who's in my class at school – she looks so sophisticated. If I couldn't have a French plaiter, I'd have someone who could tell me everything I wanted to know about boys – they're so confusing! And if I couldn't have a professor of boys, I'd be happy with someone who'd really listen to me sometimes – Dad's always so busy. Even when I try to tell him something really important he doesn't always pay attention. Like the other evening, when I made myself tell him about the three boys from Beechwood Academy who'd chased after me on the way home from school and shouted mean stuff at me, like 'We're gonna get you.'

I made myself tell Dad about it. Even though it was hard to do. The Beechwood boys had really scared me and telling Dad about it brought it all back. It was like they were in the room with us and could overhear everything I said. When I'd finished telling Dad he didn't say a word. I looked up to see why he hadn't said anything, and saw why – he'd fallen asleep!

Of course a new mum who would listen to me, and French plait my hair, and knew all about boys would be the best. But I suppose if I had to pick just one thing, then someone to talk to was the most important. Someone who'd make time for me, who'd been through it all before, who'd understand.

I looked down at the envelope I was holding. This could be our big chance.

'Let's post it,' I said to Gem.

'Okay.'

'See you in a bit, Dad,' I said, outside the bathroom. We live in a bungalow. It's better for Gem.

'Where are you going?' Dad called.

'Back in a minute.'

We set off down the street to the postbox.

'This is a bit like setting a mum trap,' Gem said, 'with Dad as the bait.'

'Yes, or going mum fishing – with a newspaper net. I hope we catch someone good.'

'I wonder how many replies Dad'll get?'

'Mmm, I wonder if he'll want to answer any of them, I hope so. He'll probably need some persuading though.'

'Fingers crossed,' said Gem.

'And toes.'

I posted the envelope into the postbox. Now all we needed to do was find someone with fingers that could French plait hair, a tongue that could tell me everything I needed to know about boys and ears that were good at listening. A picture of a lady who was all fingers, tongues and ears came into my head – not very attractive!

The *Medlock Times*, with our advert in it, dropped through the letterbox yesterday evening. I grabbed it off the doormat, before Dad saw it, and hid it in my room.

This morning we cut the advert out and put it inside Dad's birthday card. Then Gem and I made him a special birthday breakfast – boiled egg and toast.

'Let it boil for ages to make sure it's really hard, Anna,' Gem said.

'I know.'

I boiled the egg for twenty minutes before scooping it out with a spoon, dropping it into an egg cup, and chopping the top off. Then I pushed the birthday candle into the hard yellow yolk and put it on the tray, along with the rest of Dad's breakfast, on Gem's lap.

Gem pressed a button on her chair and used the joystick to steer herself down the passage. She stopped outside Dad's room.

I struck a match, lit the candle, and pushed open the door.

'Happy birthday,' we sang loudly.

Gem gave Dad his breakfast tray.

'Thanks,' he said

'Make a wish, Dad.'

Dad closed his eyes and wished. Then he blew out the candle.

I winked at Gem and gave Dad our card. As he took it I had a moment of panic. What if he didn't like our gift inside it? What if he was angry instead of pleased? I crossed my fingers as Dad tore open the envelope.

The advert fell out of the card. Dad picked it up and read it.

He didn't look cross. He looked confused.

'I don't get it,' he said. 'Is this a joke?'

I shook my head. My stomach felt funny. Maybe this wasn't going to work. Dad didn't look happy.

'But I...'

'We put the advert in for you, Dad,' Gem said. 'It's your birthday present from me and Anna.'

Dad wasn't smiling. He frowned. 'I don't like...'

'It'll be fun, Dad,' I said quickly. 'You'll probably meet someone really nice.'

Dad dropped the advert and shook his head. 'I have all the fun I need with you two, thanks very much.'

'Please, Dad,' Gem said, sounding desperate. 'You never get to go out anywhere.'

'You spend all your time with us,' I said.

'That's what dads do.'

'Please. Let's just see what replies you get before you decide whether to carry on or not,' Gem said.

'I don't like it,' Dad said. 'You shouldn't have done it without asking me first.'

'Just give it a try,' I begged him. 'You don't have to reply to any of the letters the newspaper sends on, if you don't want to.'

'Well...I don't know,' Dad said. He picked up the advert. 'It's not really...'

'Just read the replies when they come,' I urged him. 'It'd be mean not to, after someone's taken the trouble to write to you.'

Dad sighed. 'I never asked them to write to me.'

'We thought it'd make you happy,' I said.

'And we wanted a new mum,' Gem said.

Dad looked shocked. He stared at her for a few seconds. Then he turned to me. 'Do you want a new mum too?' he asked.

I nodded. 'Yes, Dad.'

He looked down at the advert. 'I don't know about this blind dating,' he said. 'It doesn't seem natural.'

'Just see who gets in touch before you decide not to, Dad,' I said.

'Go on,' said Gem. 'But you'd better tell any ladies you meet all about Anna and me.'

'They'll know about you two soon enough,' Dad said. 'You'll be coming on every meeting I go on, if I go on any at all.'

'But...' It'd be hard for Dad to be romantic with me and Gem there. How could he get amorous with us watching?

Then I realised maybe that was why Dad wanted us there.

'Otherwise all the replies can go in the bin, before I've read them,' Dad said.

'Gem and me are going to be your bodyguards!' I said.

Dad started to laugh. 'Well, I'll need some protection, if I'm going to do this daft thing,' he said. 'I don't know where you got such a crazy idea from.'

We didn't tell him it was from the 'Polly's People' show.

'I've always wanted to be a bouncer!' Gem said. 'I don't mind coming along on your dates, Dad. I'd like to see who you're going out with.' She thought for a moment and added, 'It'd be nice if she was *rich*.'

Dad didn't look amused. 'There's more important things in life than money, Gem.'

Gem looked as if she didn't quite believe him.

'Shush, Gem,' I said. I didn't want her to put Dad off the idea now he was almost going for it. Sometimes Gem said the wrong thing, without really meaning to be hurtful. She'd only been a toddler when Mum died. She couldn't remember her like me. I could remember a smiling lady who was always ready to give a hug, told great bedtime stories and kissed my knee to make it better when I fell over. She'd been gone for nearly eight years. If we could meet someone else, even a little bit like our real mum was, I'd be happy. Although someone who could French plait hair...

'How d'you really feel about this, Anna?' Dad asked me.

'I'd like us to give it a try, Dad.'

'Sure?'

'Sure.'

Dad sighed and read the advert again.

'I see you put in my age,' he said.

'All the other advertisers did,' I told him.

'And what's this bit about me being handsome and fun?'

'You are, Dad.'

'Hmm,' he said doubtfully. He patted his slightly round stomach. 'At least you didn't put my weight in the advert.' He touched the top of his head. 'And you didn't mention I'm going a bit thin on top, either. Poor ladies are going to be in for a shock when they meet me in real life, if anyone replies, and if we decide to meet them.'

'You're not that bad, Dad,' I said.

'I'm not exactly hunk of the month, though.'

10

'Maybe you'll meet a millionairess,' Gem said excitedly. 'Then I could buy one of those motor trikes and a CD player and a computer and a saxophone and...'

'Gem!' Dad said firmly. 'Someone kind who cares about us will be more than enough.'

''Course, Dad,' Gem said, and then she grinned and added, 'but I wouldn't say no if she just happened to be rich too.'

Dad sighed. 'I don't know where you get your mercenary attitude from.'

'So you will read the replies, Dad, and phone them if they sound okay?' I said.

'I don't know.'

'But you will at least read them?'

'I'll see.'

'P-l-e-a-s-e, Dad,' said Gem.

'What if something goes wrong?' Dad said.

'What could go wrong?'

'Well, we could meet someone crazy... or dangerous ... or both!'

Chapter 2

'Wake-ee, wake-ee!' Gem shouted from the kitchen, on Monday morning. 'Today could be the day we get some replies to Dad's advert!'

'Not *my* advert,' I heard Dad say. 'You're the ones who put it in the paper.'

I closed my eyes tightly, put the pillow over my head and tried hard to go back to sleep. It wasn't easy.

'Anna, breakfast's ready!' Dad yelled.

'I don't want any,' I groaned into my pillow, but my traitor of a belly didn't agree. It started to rumble.

Last night I'd decided to follow my latest copy of *Girlfriend* magazine's recommendation of exercising before breakfast. But this morning my body didn't even want to move. Exercise was something it did more than enough of during PE at school, thanks very much. It'd probably go on strike if I started exercising at home too.

The smell of sizzling bacon wafted into my room and I climbed out of bed, had a very fast shower, threw on my school uniform and hurried to the kitchen.

Some of Dad's meals turn out a bit strange. But his breakfast making's always the best.

'Morning, sleepyhead,' Dad said, handing me a plate of bacon, mushrooms, tomatoes and beans.

I sat down at the kitchen table and tucked in, only remembering with the tiniest pang of guilt *Girlfriend*'s other recommendation of a bowl of cereal, followed by a large glass of freshly squeezed juice, for breakfast.

It was too hard to follow the magazine's instructions so early in the morning. Anyway, the same article had also encouraged plenty of beauty sleep, but Dad wasn't going to let me miss school and stay in bed all morning, just because *Girlfriend* said I could!

Sometimes he even gets a little bit cross when I quote him stuff from my magazine. He says *Girlfriend*'s a waste of money. He doesn't understand that I need it – how else am I going to get all that vital information?

I was squeezing some ketchup on the side of my plate when the doorbell rang.

'That'll be Tina,' Gem said. 'I've got to go. See you later, alligators.'

'What are you setting off to school so early for?' Dad asked.

'Things to do,' Gem said, mysteriously.

'Be good,' said Dad.

'I always am!' Gem retorted.

'Really?' Dad said, his voice heavy with disbelief.

'Almost always, then,' Gem said.

Dad had gone ballistic when Gem came home with her hair sprayed green the other week. He only calmed down after she told him it'd be gone as soon as she washed her hair.

'See ya,' Gem laughed. ''Bye, Anna.'

I made a ''bye' sort of sound, around a mouthful of toast.

Gem pressed a button on her chair and glided out into the hall.

'Hi,' I heard her say to Tina, and then the front door closed.

A few seconds later the bell rang again. Gem must have forgotten something. I stopped eating and stood up.

The bell rang again and kept on ringing. Then there was a banging – a banging that sounded like someone kicking the front door.

Gem couldn't kick the door – even if she wanted to. So who was it?

Dad looked out of the window.

'Oh no!' he said.

'Help! Help! Let me in!' a female voice shouted.

I dropped my toast, ran to the front door and yanked it open. A woman, wearing a postwoman's uniform, with black hair – cropped very very short – and skull and crossbone earrings in her ears, leapt past me into the passage.

'Shut it! Shut it!' she shouted, pointing to the door.

'Huh?'

She slammed the front door closed and collapsed against the hall table.

A moment later I heard what sounded like a huge dog, or even maybe a wolf, although I'd only heard them on the TV, so didn't know exactly what they sounded like in real life, begin to howl outside the door.

I looked over at the postwoman. What was chasing her?

'Lucky you opened the door when you did,' she gasped. 'You were only just in time, another second and I'd have been mincemeat. All I was trying to do was deliver a letter to a house round the corner – the next second it came tearing after me – as if I was public enemy number one.'

Dad came out into the hall. He looked like he was trying hard not to laugh.

I thought it was very rude of him to be smiling at a time like this. No way was it a laughing matter. The postwoman could have been seriously injured. The dog-wolf thing had stopped howling now, but I didn't even like to think about what might have happened if it had got its teeth into her.

I could tell the postwoman wasn't very impressed with Dad's smiling, trying-hard-not-to-laugh face, either. She frowned at him and opened her mouth to say something...

But the doorbell rang again, making me jump and the postwoman scream.

Dad's hand stretched out to open the door.

'Don't...' the postwoman and I cried together.

But it was too late.

'Dogs don't ring doorbells,' Dad said, and he opened the door.

Outside stood old Mr Harris. He's rumoured to be a hundred – and he looks at least that old. The kids all call him Gummy Harris because he's always losing his false teeth, leaving him only his shiny pink gums to mush his food with.

Once someone found his false teeth under a chair in the library and another time they were spotted at the bottom of the local swimming pool.

He lost his last pair of false teeth a few weeks ago and hasn't got round to replacing them yet. 'They'll turn up soon,' he'd say, whenever anyone suggested buying a new pair. But so far they hadn't.

'Hello, Mr Harris,' I said, from behind the safety of Dad's back. I stared at the huge, fierce-looking dog he was holding by its chain collar.

'Sorry about Rambo,' Mr Harris said, nodding at the postwoman, who was standing behind me, well back. 'He got a little bit over-excited.'

'Over-excited!' the postwoman squeaked. 'I thought he was going to tear me to bits!'

'That's just it, my dear,' said Gummy Harris. 'He couldn't have.'

'Well, he had a good try,' I said. 'Poor...' I looked over at the postwoman, not sure what to call her.

'Kate,' the postwoman supplied.

'Poor Kate was scared half to death.'

Dad burst out laughing.

Kate gave Dad a look that would have turned him into a frog, if looks could do that sort of thing.

'Shut up, Dad,' I said. He doesn't usually go around laughing at other people's misfortunes.

Dad tried hard to stop, but he didn't totally succeed. The laughter looked like it could burst out of him at any moment.

'Yes, but he couldn't have hurt her, not really,' Mr

Harris said.

I stared at Rambo. He might be sitting docilely at Mr Harris's feet now, but what about the hungry, ferocious-sounding wolf howls I'd heard only a few seconds ago?

'He's all bluff,' Mr Harris said, looking down at Rambo fondly. 'Even if he had caught up with you er... Kate, all he'd have been able to do was lick you and I've never heard of anyone being licked to death before.'

'But...'

'No teeth, my dear, like me,' Mr Harris said, and he opened Rambo's mouth to show Kate and me Rambo's gums. 'That's why I brought him home from the dog shelter yesterday. They were going to have him put down, but I said I'd have him, because he reminds me of me.' Then he chuckled and winked at Kate. 'Not that I'd have had the puff to chase after you like Rambo did. I'd better leave that to you younger chaps.' He winked at Dad.

Dad looked embarrassed.

'I think I'd rather have your dog chasing me,' Kate said, staring daggers at Dad.

Rambo didn't look scary now we knew he didn't have any teeth to bite or rip with.

Kate went to pet him.

'Your bark really is a lot worse than your bite,' she told him. 'But I'm very pleased to know there's no need to be frightened of you anymore and we can be friends.'

Rambo licked Kate's nose.

'How did you know Rambo didn't have any teeth?' I asked Dad.

'I met him and Mr Harris out walking yesterday evening,' Dad said.

I went to stroke Rambo too.

'Me and Rambo had better be off,' Gummy Harris said. 'We've had enough excitement for one morning.'

Slowly, with the dog leading, Mr Harris and Rambo headed for home.

'Would you like a cup of tea?' Dad said to Kate.

Big mistake. Kate was still furious with him for laughing at her terror.

'No, I wouldn't,' she said. 'I've had more than enough of your company to last me a lifetime.' She thrust her hand into her postbag and drew out a Manila packet. 'Your post,' she said, slapping it down on the hall table.

'I'm so...' Dad started to say.

I didn't blame Kate for feeling cross with him. 'It was really rude of you to laugh at Kate being frightened of Rambo, Dad,' I said.

Dad's face twitched and the next second he burst out laughing again. 'S-sorry,' he gasped, clutching his stomach. 'It was just so funny.'

'Goodbye,' Kate said, icily. She stormed out of the bungalow and along the path.

'Dad!' I said. What had got into him? His sense of humour was really warped.

I grabbed my school bag and ran after Kate. I had to apologise for Dad's behaviour.

'Wait up!' I called after her. She didn't stop. But I caught up with her anyway.

'I'm sorry about my dad,' I said. 'He's not usually like that.'

'Hmm,' Kate said.

'Are you going back to the sorting office?' I asked.

'Yes.'

'Oh good,' I said. 'That's on my way to school. I'll walk with you.'

Kate didn't say anything. I could tell she was getting less angry as we walked though, because I didn't have to jog to keep up with her.

We overtook Gummy Harris. Rambo wagged his tail.

'Have you been a postwoman long?' I asked Kate.

'Nope, today was my first day delivering letters.'

'Do you think you'll like being a postwoman?'

Kate shrugged. 'Uniform jobs run in my family. My sister's a firefighter and my brother's a policeman.' She touched the skull and crossbone earrings she was wearing. 'My brother gave me these earrings. I wore them today to bring me luck.' Suddenly she smiled and added, 'Maybe they did bring me luck – at least Rambo didn't have any teeth.'

'Yes, that was lucky,' I agreed.

'Your mum should teach your dad that it's not polite to laugh at other people's terror,' Kate said.

'Mum died when I was five and my sister, Gem, was almost two,' I told her. For years after the accident I'd had nightmares about it. It happened on a sunny day. Dad had been driving us to the beach. I was sitting in the back seat. Gem was on Mum's lap in the front.

The car that hit us had been going so fast it didn't

19

have time to stop. It smashed into the passenger door. Into Mum and Gem.

I didn't want to talk about the accident.

For a few seconds we walked in silence. Then Kate said, 'Has your dad seen other people since...?'

I shook my head. Then found myself telling Kate all about the lonely hearts advert we'd put in the paper for Dad's birthday present.

'That's a great idea,' Kate said. Then she added, 'You know you might have got some replies today. The packet I left on your hall table was from the *Medlock Times*.'

'Was it!'

We reached my school.

'See you,' I said.

'Good luck with the advert,' said Kate. 'I'll keep my fingers crossed for someone really nice. Just don't let your dad laugh at them if they trip up, or have spinach in their teeth, or something. Dates don't like being laughed at.'

'Okay.'

It was hard to concentrate at school. All I wanted to think about, apart from Leo, who's this boy in my class I'm always thinking about, was the possibility that one of the replies on the hall table might belong to the lady who'd become my new mum. A new mum who could French plait my hair, tell me all about boys, and listen when I needed to talk.

Chapter 3

'This year's school disco will be held on Friday the 17th,' Mrs Trent said, and I immediately stopped thinking about the lonely heart advert replies and started to think about the disco instead.

It was only for pupils in year 8 and up, so this was the first year I could go.

Behind me, I heard Jenny Carter, of French plait fame, whisper to Sarah, who was sitting next to her, 'I'm going with Robert – who're you going with?'

'Ben,' Sarah whispered back. Of course! Dates for the disco. My chance – if I was brave enough – to ask Leo out.

I looked over at him. He was sitting at the back of the classroom. His head bent, as usual, over a computer magazine. Would he ask me to the disco if I didn't ask him?

I knew the answer was no.

Could I be brave and ask him out, then? I knew I couldn't. Don't get me wrong, I wanted to – badly – but it was too hard.

And anyway he might say no. *No*, he wasn't going to the disco, or *no* he always went to his gran's on Friday nights, or worst of all, *no* he didn't want to go with me

– because he was already going with someone else.

What if I wrote him a note? That wouldn't be so hard. I could do that.

I tore the middle pages out of my maths book and put my arm around the paper, so no one could see what I was writing. My hand shook a bit as I wrote:

'Dear Leo,
> Would you like to go to the disco with me,
> because I'd like to go with you?
Anna'

At the bottom I put my address and phone number.

When I'd written the note I wasn't sure what to do with it. Should I try to hand it to him? Or would it be better to sneak it into his bag?

If I handed it to him I'd get a reply straight away – but I'd have to make sure no one was around to overhear us. I'd feel so awful if he said no.

I needed to wait for the right moment.

It took a long time coming. I didn't get a chance to see Leo alone, and give him the note, before break. And I couldn't catch him at breaktime because he went to computer club and I'm not in it this term.

I tried smiling at him during music in the second half of the morning, but he only looked surprised and then frowned a lot.

He didn't know how I felt about him yet – because I'd only realised it myself last week. He'd find out soon enough.

I know some people might think Leo's a slightly

unusual love choice, but my tummy does funny flips whenever I'm near him. My magazine, *Girlfriend*, says tummy flipping is one of the ways you can tell if a boy's special or not.

Dad would probably have said my tummy flipping was indigestion. But I know it isn't. I know it's true love, only of course, Leo doesn't know yet.

I kept looking at him in the dining hall at lunch time. But all he did was check behind him to see if I was looking at someone else and then avoid making eye contact.

'He's shy,' I told myself, and decided that perhaps it'd be better secretly to drop the note into his bag for him to find when he got home.

My chance to deposit the note came later in the afternoon, in biology. Miss Marks gave us this truly disgusting experiment to do. It was to see how much bacteria there is in saliva.

While Leo was taking his full test tube of saliva to show Miss Marks, I knelt down beside his bag and pretended to be tying my shoe lace. It was surprisingly easy to slip my note into the pocket of his bag without anyone seeing.

Mission accomplished I went back to my place and carried on spitting into my test tube. Now all I had to do was wait for Leo's reply.

I kept watch for the rest of the afternoon, but as far as I could tell he didn't look in the pocket of his bag.

''Bye, Leo,' I said, at the end of the day.

'Er... 'bye,' was his startled response.

I hoped he'd find my note very soon.

I ran out of school and almost the whole way home, until I got a stitch and had to walk for a bit. I couldn't wait to grab the packet of lonely heart letters and show them to Dad and Gem.

'At last!' Gem said, as I came bursting through the back door.

Five envelopes lay, waiting, on the kitchen table. The brown packet, they'd been sent in from the newspaper, lay on the side.

I sat down in the third chair and grinned at Dad and Gem. Maybe our new mum was waiting amongst the letters on the table.

'This is it,' I said.

'We haven't opened any of the letters, yet,' Dad said.

'It's been murder waiting for you to get here,' Gem complained. 'I told Dad you wouldn't mind if I just opened one.'

'And I said you *would* mind. So we waited,' Dad said.

'But we don't have to wait anymore! Can I open the first one and read it out?' Gem looked at Dad and me and then added, 'As I've had to wait *forever* just staring at the envelopes.'

'Okay,' said Dad.

'Sure,' I nodded.

Gem picked up a blue envelope and tore it open.

'Two pages,' she said, holding up the sheets of paper covered in large, very round writing.

'We're ready,' I said, and crossed my fingers. Please let this be her, I thought.

Gem started to read:

'Hi, Handsome and Fun Widower
with two daughters,'

Dad groaned, 'I'm not handsome or fun. She'll be in for a shock if she meets me.'

'Ssh, Dad,' I said.

Gem continued:

'My name's Sue – Rodeo Sue. I'm 40 years old and 1.65 metres tall.

I'm not particularly attractive, but I'm not so bad I need to wear a paper bag over my head either.

Do you or your lovely daughters ride?

I own a beautiful palomino mare called Tara. There's nothing better than an early morning gallop to chase away the blues, especially when you've caught the man you thought you were in love with, with his lips stuck to another woman's.

I work for the Wild West theme park over in Leaston. I've put in three complimentary tickets for you and your daughters to come to the theme park and show, Saturday week – hope you can make it. I'll be looking out for you.

Sue

P.S. How about meeting up in the Cowhands Café after the show?'

'She sounds great!' Gem said. 'I can't wait to meet her horse.'

'Yeah,' I agreed. Although I wanted to meet Rodeo Sue more than her horse. Rodeo Sue was sure to know how to French plait hair, and I bet she could tell me all about boys, and listen to me when I needed to talk. Rodeo Sue sounded like ideal mum material. Just perfect.

'I'm not sure,' said Dad.

My heart sank. 'Why not?' I asked him.

He picked up Rodeo Sue's letter. 'It's the bit where she writes about finding the man she thought she was in love with kissing someone else. I don't think she's over him yet, not by a long way. And another thing . . . ' Dad's face went a bit pink.

'What?' Gem and I said.

'I don't really like horses. They're so big and they have these huge biting teeth. I used to have nightmares about them when I was a kid.'

'Oh, Dad,' Gem laughed. 'There's nothing to be scared of. Horses don't eat meat.'

'I still don't like them,' Dad said.

'Shall we make a yes, no, and not sure pile?' I said.

'Okay, let's put Rodeo Sue's letter in the not sure pile.' Dad looked relieved.

'But I want to go to the theme park and rodeo show,' I said. 'We have to meet her. It'd be rude not to go to the show after she's sent us free tickets.'

'Yes, we have to go to the Wild West theme park,' Gem said.

Dad sighed and swopped Sue's letter from the not

sure to the yes pile. 'Just don't let any horses bite me, okay?' he said.

'Okay,' we promised, although Gem and I hadn't had much to do with horses. Neither of us had ever been riding. The nearest I'd been to a horse was when I'd fed one some grass over a fence. Horses didn't really bite people, did they? And if one did try to bite Dad, how were we supposed to stop it?

'Your turn next, Dad,' I said.

'Which one shall I choose?' Dad said, staring at the four remaining letters. 'This one I think.'

He picked up the smallest of the envelopes and opened it. Inside was a miniature hand-drawn card.

'I like this,' said Dad. The hand-drawn picture on the front of the card was of a fireman stuck in a chimney. It wasn't the greatest drawing in the world, but the expression on the fireman's face was very funny.

'Kate's sister's a firefighter,' I said.

'Who's Kate?' Gem asked.

'Our new post lady. She took refuge in our house when a huge dog chased her this morning.'

'I miss all the good things,' Gem said.

'The *huge* dog turned out to have no teeth,' Dad told her.

'Dad's in disgrace for laughing at her,' I said.

'The postwoman or the dog?' Gem asked.

'The postwoman. The dog's a he. His name's Rambo and Gummy Harris rescued him from the dog centre,' I told her.

'I didn't mean to laugh at the postwoman,' Dad said. 'I don't know what came over me. The harder I tried not to laugh, the more I did. I just couldn't help it.'

'I don't think Kate'll ever forgive you,' I said, remembering her furious face.

Dad changed the subject. 'This fireman card looks promising.' He opened it and read aloud:

> 'Dear Widower with two daughters,
> My name's Bibi. I'm a Leo, 33 years old and never been married.
>
> I like having fun and laughing, but can be serious too.
>
> Your advert didn't mention what you do, so I decided to imagine you were a fireman and drew you this card.
>
> I'd really like to hear from you, but if you decide not to reply then I wish you lots of luck and happiness with whoever you do choose to contact.
>
> All the best
> Bibi xxx
> 01003 786523'

'She's going to be disappointed when she finds out I'm not a fireman, but an accountant,' Dad said. He put the little card back in its envelope. Then looked at me and Gem.

'Yes!' we said.

'I don't . . .' Dad said.

'Yes, yes, yes,' Gem and I insisted.

'Okay,' Dad sighed, and he put Bibi's card in the yes pile.

Bibi sounded great. Just as good mum material as Sue. Maybe even better. There were no horses for Dad to get worried about with Bibi.

'My turn,' I said. I picked up an envelope and tore it open.

> 'Dear Man with two daughters,
> You must be very lonely without a woman in your life. I can move in straight away.
> Why not give me a call?
> Frances
> 01003 927658'

'Uh-oh,' I said.

'The no pile,' Dad said, quickly. 'She sounds scary!'

'I wonder if a lot of scary people answer newspaper adverts,' Gem said.

'The rest of the letters weren't scary,' I said.

'Two left to choose from,' Dad said. 'Your turn, Gem.'

Gem chose a Manila envelope and carefully tore it open.

> 'Dear Widower with two daughters,
> My name's Janet and I'm 39 years old. I have one daughter, Olivia. She's 14, a star in the making, and the most precious jewel in my life. Her father and I are separated.
> Why don't we all meet up in town for a pizza or something and a

friendly, getting-to-know-each-other chat?
Janet
01003 876090'

'She sounds okay,' Dad said, 'a nice, regular sort of woman.'

'I'm not sure about her daughter being a *star in the making and a precious jewel*,' I said. Olivia sounded a bit sick making.

'I like pizzas,' Gem said.

'The yes pile,' Dad decided.

Janet didn't sound as good mum material as Sue and Bibi, but Gem put Janet's letter into the yes pile.

'You open the last one, Anna,' Dad said.

I picked up the last envelope and opened it.

'Dear Widower with two daughters,
My name is Elaine and I'm 37 years old. I've been a widow for the last three years.

As you can imagine, life has been very difficult for my fourteen-year-old son and me recently, but I think it's now time to make myself meet new people and go out again.

I hope you will get in contact.

It would be good to have someone to talk to.

Elaine
01003-765587'

'I have to get in touch with her,' Dad said. 'Even if we don't go out with her. She sounds like she needs someone to talk to badly.'

'Okay,' said Gem.

I put Elaine's letter into the yes pile. I wasn't sure if I'd like having a step-brother a year older than me. It could be excellent if he was really nice. It could be awful if he wasn't.

Was Dad thinking of Elaine as one of his dates or as someone who needed to have a chat about being a widow?

'That's all the letters,' Gem said.

It was a shame we hadn't caught more possible mums in our mum trap. But we only needed one mum and maybe Sue or Bibi, Janet or Elaine would be the one. I hoped so.

'Now,' Dad said, 'you must both be starving. Would you like me to make dinner, or shall I phone our *yeses* before we have something to eat?'

We were too excited to eat.

'Phone them,' said Gem.

'This one first,' I said, picking out Rodeo Sue's letter.

Dad looked at the letter, turned it over, and then said, 'She hasn't put her phone number on this.'

I took the letter back. 'I suppose she only wants to meet us if we want to go to the theme park,' I said.

'And we do want to, don't we?' said Gem.

'Yes,' I said, enthusiastically.

'Yes,' said Dad, less enthusiastically.

'Next one,' said Gem, handing Dad Bibi's card.

31

'Okay,' Dad said. 'I'd better phone before I get scared and chicken out. You are sure you want me to do this?'

'Yes,' Gem and I said.

Dad lifted the telephone receiver and dialled the number.

I leant close to Dad so I could hear both sides of the conversation.

The phone rang six times and then there was the sound of an answering machine clicking on.

'Hi, I can't come to the phone at the moment. Please leave your message and phone number and I'll call you back as soon as I can,' said a friendly, husky, female voice.

Dad put the receiver down.

'Answer machine.'

'Leave a message,' I said.

'I think I'll try again after dinner,' Dad said. 'I'd rather speak to her in person than leave a message.'

I gave Dad Janet's letter.

He dialled her number. It rang three times.

'Hello?' said a girl's voice.

'Hello,' said Dad, 'is that Janet?'

'No. Mum!' yelled the voice.

'Doesn't sound much like a precious jewel,' I whispered.

Dad bit his bottom lip. He looked scared.

'Hello?'

'Hello,' Dad said, 'you replied to my advert. I'm the man with two daughters.'

'Oh, hello. I was hoping you'd call,' Janet said. Her

voice sounded warm and friendly on the phone. Dad and she chatted for a while and then they arranged for all five of us to meet at the Pizza Palace for lunch on Saturday.

'My daughter, Olivia, might know one of your daughters. What schools do they go to?' Janet asked.

'St John's High and Aylands Primary,' Dad said.

'Oh, Olivia goes to Beechwood Academy – for exceptional children. She's very talented you know.'

I felt pretty sure I wasn't going to like Olivia much.

'Roll on Saturday!' said Gem. 'I love pizza. I'm going to order the most expens...'

I nudged Gem, who changed what she was going to say to '...a reasonably priced, average-sized pizza. In fact, I might only want a small cheese and tomato one.'

Next Dad dialled Elaine's number.

'Hello...is that Elaine...you replied to my ad. Yes...yes.'

I leaned closer. Elaine had a quiet voice and I could only just hear what she said.

'How about Sunday?' Elaine's whispery voice said. 'Around eleven o'clock? Is there anywhere that you, or your daughters, particularly like to go to?'

Dad looked at Gem. 'Anywhere you'd like to go?'

'Fifty Flavours, Fifty Flavours,' she said urgently.

'Well,' Dad said, into the phone, 'there is the Fifty Flavours Ice Cream Bar?'

Elaine said she'd see us there.

Gem put her thumbs up. 'Yes!'

'I'll try and persuade my son to come along, but I

don't know if he will or not. I'll be there, though – with
or without him.'

'Right,' said Dad. 'See you then.'

He put the phone down. 'Now we've done it,' he said.
He looked more worried than pleased.

Chapter 4

'I haven't got anything to wear,' Gem complained loudly, on Saturday morning.

I knew how she felt. When I'd opened my wardrobe I found all my clothes had suddenly turned too old-fashioned, too small, or too young.

'Hideous...gross...revolting...' I muttered to myself as my fingers passed, with disgust, over clothes that had been fine yesterday, but were hateful today.

I'd never impress Olivia or Janet, with clothes like these. Olivia was sure to own all the latest fashions. She'd look fantastic in anything she wore. I hadn't seen what she looked like of course, but she sounded exactly like that sort of girl.

Unlike me, I thought, throwing clothes onto my bed. If I wore a potato sack I'd look like a sack of potatoes, if Olivia wore one she'd probably look like a fashion model.

I heard Dad go into Gem's room, next to mine.

'What about this?' he said.

'Too old.'

'How about this, then?'

'It's got a hole in it.'

'You used to look great in this.'

35

'Yes – when I was about five!'

'There's nothing to worry about,' Dad sighed. 'Janet and Olivia are just people, like us, they're not royalty.'

Yes, but they might be going to become part of our family, I thought to myself. Janet might become our new mum, Olivia our step-sister. It was suddenly all very scary.

'I know they're not *royalty*,' Gem agreed. 'I feel much more nervous than if we were going to meet the Queen!'

'We don't have to meet them, if you don't want to,' Dad said. 'I never thought it was a good idea anyway. If you like I could phone and cancel. Then we could have a nice, peaceful Saturday, instead.'

'No way – we're meeting them!' I shouted, through the wall.

Our mum trap would never work if we let Dad cancel the dates.

'I'll wear this,' Gem decided quickly.

I pulled on a pair of jeans and a shirt that had been my favourite, up until this morning.

'Yes, you look revolting,' I told my reflection in the mirror. Then stared at my face in horror. That couldn't be a spot coming up on my chin, could it? A glaring, staring, impossible-not-to-notice spot! Just what I didn't need! I hid it, as best I could, beneath a mountain of make-up.

Hoping no one would notice my spot I went downstairs, picked up an old copy of *Girlfriend*, and flicked through it.

I was soon engrossed, apart from a nervous worry

about Olivia and Janet every few seconds, in a test on how to tell if your boyfriend *really* loves you.

Ten minutes later Dad collapsed on the sofa beside me. 'We all just need to relax,' he said. 'This is supposed to be fun, not torture.'

'My hair looks like a lot of rats' tails,' Gem groaned, gliding into the room.

'How about clipping it up?' Dad said.

'*And* I've got a whole family of butterflies living in my stomach.'

'Me too,' Dad admitted.

'My butterflies are having sword fights,' I said.

Too soon it was time to meet Janet and Olivia.

'This is it,' Dad said, as we went out of the front door.

'I hope they like us,' I said.

Dad shrugged. 'If they don't, there's plenty more fish in the sea.'

'What are you talking about *fish* for?' Gem asked, looking confused. 'I thought we were having pizza.'

'What I mean is, if we don't like Janet and her daughter, or they don't like us, then there's lots more people out there for us to meet,' Dad said.

'Oh.'

I crossed my fingers and hoped that Janet and Olivia would turn out to be people we could like and perhaps more importantly, who'd like us. If Janet did seem right for the position of mum, how soon could I ask her if she could do French plaits? Maybe Olivia could do one – I was sure she'd be able to – I was sure Olivia could do everything.

We arrived at the Pizza Palace and waited outside, trying not to look too anxious, trying to look as if we were always meeting strange people outside restaurants.

'What if they don't turn up?' I said.

'We'll still have a pizza,' Dad said.

'I hope they get here soon,' said Gem.

'I think that's them,' I said, looking at a woman and a girl, a bit older than me, coming towards us. The girl looked vaguely familiar. But I couldn't think where I'd seen her before.

Gem waved.

'Tony, Anna and Gem I presume,' the lady said. 'I'm Janet and this is my daughter, Olivia.'

We all shook hands.

Olivia was wearing the latest fashion, had a great figure, great hair, great skin and perfect teeth.

I wondered what she thought about me. Probably not a lot.

I smiled at her and she half smiled back. Then touched her own chin in exactly the same place the spot was on mine.

'Is that peanut butter?' she asked.

'No, no,' I said, furiously rubbing at my chin. I knew I shouldn't have put on so much make-up.

'Shall we go in?' Dad said.

Gem expertly steered her chair inside.

My chin felt raw where I'd rubbed at it. My spot was probably glaring out at the world like an angry eye.

A waiter led us to a table in the corner and took away one of the chairs.

'Well, this is nice,' Janet said, as we sat down.

She sounded like she was lying.

I tried, but just couldn't stop staring at Olivia. She was only a little bit older than me but she acted three million times more sophisticated.

Why can't I be more like her? I thought, as I read through my menu.

'You might have seen Olivia on TV recently,' Janet said. 'She's starring in the advert for Sweet Stuff.'

'Oh – that's where I've seen you, then,' I said, remembering the advert where hundreds of people chewed Sweet Stuff, the new chewy sweet, in unison.

Olivia shrugged. 'I'm hoping to get a part on "Charm" soon.'

'Are you?' I said, very impressed. 'Charm' is a new soap opera about a group of really glamorous teenagers – who don't look like normal teenagers at all – they go to St Chalmers school – which they call Charm.

'Olivia's got an audition next week,' Janet said, proudly.

I nodded. I wasn't surprised. Olivia would fit right into the 'Charm' image.

'You said you'd recently moved here?' Dad said to Janet, when the pizzas arrived.

'Yes,' Janet said, 'I moved for Olivia's sake, really. I wanted her to go to Beechwood Academy. It has such a good reputation. Nothing's too good for my daughter. And there was another reason.' Suddenly Janet looked very angry.

'What?' Dad asked.

'I can hardly bring myself to talk about it, it's so awful.'

This sounded really interesting.

'What?' I asked.

'The school accused Olivia of being a bully – I was outraged, as you can imagine. My daughter would never do a thing like that. It's not in her nature.'

'Shall I cut your pizza up for you?' Olivia said to Gem.

'No, I . . .'

'That's very sweet of you, Olivia,' Janet said.

'But I don't need anyone to cut up my pizza – I can do it myself,' Gem said.

Janet didn't listen. 'You can see why I was so shocked when they said my daughter had been caught bullying.'

Olivia tried to cut up Gem's pizza. Gem pushed her away.

'Olivia's always been very kind, especially considering she's an only child. Only children aren't supposed to be willing to share, are they? But my Olivia's generous to a fault. I call her my little angel,' Janet said.

I looked at Gem. Gem made a being sick face. I made one back.

Janet and Olivia were too much!

Luckily they didn't see our being sick faces, but Dad did.

'I've always wondered what it would be like to have sisters,' Olivia said, smiling full force at Gem and me.

Gem almost choked on her piece of pizza.

You're not going to find out by living with us, I thought. We didn't want to catch a mum in our mum trap *that* badly.

'We'll have to do this again, sometime,' Janet said, when we'd all finished eating.

'Mmm, yes,' Dad said.

No thank you, I thought. Even if Janet was a champion French plaiter, boy informer and listener I wouldn't want her for my mum.

Gem's face told me she didn't want to catch Janet in our mum trap either.

On the way home we stopped at the newsagent's. I bought my regular copy of *Girlfriend*. Gem bought a packet of Sweet Stuff. Each of us took a sweet and started chewing.

'Too sickly,' we decided.

'So what did you think about our first date?' Dad asked, when we were back home.

'Yuck,' said Gem.

'I don't want to have to meet them again,' I said.

'Me, neither,' Dad agreed and switched the kettle on. 'I don't think this blind dating thing is going to work.'

'Yes it will,' said Gem.

'We just have to meet the right person,' I told him.

'So you didn't fancy having Olivia as a step-sister?' Dad said, when he'd made the tea.

'No way!'

Later in the afternoon Gem and Dad went swimming, as usual. Sometimes I go with them, but more often I stay at home, watch TV, read *Girlfriend*, and have the whole place to myself for a change.

''Bye, Anna,' Gem called.

''Bye.'

As soon as I heard the front door close I grabbed my copy of *Girlfriend*, and turned to the centre pages.

The article was called 'Be Naturally Beautiful'. It explained how food could be used to transform an ordinary-looking skin into a radiant one.

I very much wanted a radiant skin. But the only thing that was radiating was the spot on my chin. It was growing much too fast!

'Nature has the answer to the quest for beautiful skin,' the article began. It went on to list the ingredients for four different face masks, all guaranteed to leave the skin healthy and glowing.

The first one consisted of beaten egg whites. Uurgh! Raw eggs were too revolting even to think about – let alone smooth all over my face – what if some went into my mouth by mistake, or got on my lips and then I accidentally licked my lips, and then...no, no, no!

Not even for Leo could I eat any part of a raw egg.

Although I wouldn't have cared if Leo had been forced to eat a raw egg. He must have found my note, when he got home on Monday, but all week he'd kept acting as if he hadn't. Him not even bothering to reply to me was almost worse than him finding my note and saying, 'No way!'

I'd glared at him on Tuesday, Wednesday, Thursday and Friday, but all he'd done was look confused. Boys!

I've decided that he's slime and doesn't deserve me – even with a big spot on my chin.

The second suggested face mask was mashed banana. I looked in the fruit bowl but there was only a couple of sad looking apples left.

Honey and oatmeal face mask then – only was oatmeal the same as porridge oats, or was it something else?

Avocado – that was the one. I'd seen an avocado lurking in the back of our fridge a couple of days ago.

I opened the fridge and took the avocado out.

It looked a bit sorry for itself and had gone very soft, but that wouldn't matter, it needed to be mashed.

I cut the avocado in half and tore away the skin. Smears of avocado got up my nails. I didn't want to get any in my hair when I spread it over my face. I grabbed a pair of knickers from the clean washing basket. They made an excellent head band. I took out a towel too and put it round my neck. Then finished mashing the avocado and smeared as much of it as I could over my face. It looked quite a lot like green sick. I might not look attractive but at least I knew it was doing my skin good.

I sat down at the kitchen table to wait for the clock on the wall to tick away the fifteen minutes I was supposed to leave the avocado mask on for. I'd have liked a drink but the face mask felt as though it might slip off my face if I moved too much.

I closed my eyes and tried to relax à la *Girlfriend*'s instructions.

When the doorbell rang I almost fell off the chair. Who was ringing the doorbell? Now was definitely not a good time to be visiting.

Could it be Gem and Dad? No, they wouldn't be back this soon from swimming and anyway, one of them would have a key.

I couldn't not answer it, but what about my face? I didn't want to wash the mask off quickly and then find out the bellringer was only someone mucking about – playing knock-door-run.

Better to look through the spyhole and check who it was first.

I kept my face tilted upwards as I walked to the door.

On the other side of the spyhole stood someone very familiar. Someone I wasn't expecting. Leo.

What was he doing here? He lived over the other side of town.

Once, in my dreams, he'd rung the doorbell and declared he couldn't live without me. But this was reality, this was Saturday afternoon, and I was wearing an avocado face mask that looked like green vomit.

I couldn't let him see me like this!

But if I ran to the bathroom and washed it off he'd think I wasn't in, and go, and might not come back. And if I tried to wipe it off with the towel I might miss some of it, and little bits of green, sick-looking stuff stuck to my face would look almost as bad as being covered in it.

The doorbell rang again and I knew I had to answer the door fast.

I took the towel from around my neck and put it over my head. The only problem was now I couldn't see Leo, but that was too bad.

I opened the door.

'Hello, Leo.' My voice sounded a bit muffled from inside the towel.

'Anna?'

'Yes.'

'Why've you got a towel over your head?'

What did he have to be so nosy for? Why did he think I'd got a towel over my head? And what lie could I tell him, because I certainly wasn't going to tell him the truth? He'd never understand. Boys wouldn't!

Then I remembered Leo was in disgrace. He hadn't even replied to my note inviting him to be my partner at the school disco.

'What do you want, Leo?' I said.

'Er – about your note.'

'Yes.'

'Yes, please.'

'Yes, please, what?'

'Yes, please, I'd like to go to the disco with you and I'll pick you up at seven thirty.'

I was so amazed I almost pulled the towel off my head. But remembered what my face looked like, just in time.

'Right,' I said.

'Right, 'bye.'

I waited for a while, not sure how long it would take Leo to walk up the path and out of the gate, not sure if anyone else was walking past, wondering why I was standing at the front door with a yellow towel over my head.

But underneath the towel I was smiling. Leo said yes!!!

For the rest of the day I went round in a love daze. *Girlfriend* said it was perfectly normal to act dreamily when you'd found your one true love. Dad told me to snap out of it – just because I accidentally put a little salt, instead of sugar, in his tea. I suppose I shouldn't have expected Dad to understand. Love dazes must be a thing only women get – just one more reason why I need a new mum. She'd be able to tell me all about things like love dazes.

Janet was out of the running, but maybe Elaine would be right.

Chapter 5

After breakfast on Sunday it was time to get ready for our second date from the newspaper. Today we were going to meet Elaine and her son at the Fifty Flavours Ice Cream Bar.

When I opened my wardrobe I was amazed to find that my clothes had changed back into being okay clothes overnight. They weren't all the latest fashion, true, but they weren't totally hopeless, either.

Gem must have felt the same way about her own clothes because I didn't hear her complaining she had nothing to wear.

The hours before the date slipped by much more peacefully than the ones before yesterday's date had done.

'I don't feel at all scared today,' Gem said, pushing the remote control button to switch on the TV.

'Me, neither.'

'We're starting to get used to this blind dating thing already,' Dad said. 'But I still don't think we're going to find you a new mum or me a new wife from it.'

'We might,' Gem said.

'We will,' I said. 'Elaine and her son have got to be better than Janet and Olivia.'

'Yeah, nobody could be as bad as them,' Gem agreed.

'Don't bet on it,' said Dad.

At half past ten we left for the date.

'I think I'll have a strawberry shortcake ice cream,' Gem said.

'Toffee fudge,' I decided.

'Double chocolate truffle,' said Dad. 'Heaven.'

We'd almost reached the Fifty Flavours Ice Cream Bar before my stomach butterflies woke up and started jumping about like fleas.

'I wonder what Elaine and her son, if he comes with her, will be like?' I said, starting to feel nervous. 'We don't even know his name.'

'She sounded pretty doubtful that her son would come,' Dad said. 'So it'll probably only be Elaine.'

But as we approached the ice cream bar I saw it wasn't only Elaine.

A boy of about fourteen and a woman, wearing a beige mac, stood outside the ice cream bar.

I felt sick. I knew the boy. Well, not exactly knew him, but I'd met him and I didn't want to have to meet him again. He was one of the boys from Beechwood Academy that had picked on me after school. I didn't know how I was going to talk to him. I didn't even want to be anywhere near him.

I knew he and his mum had to be our date, and I no longer wanted to be on it. I wanted to be back at home. Nice and safe.

The boy saw me, looked shocked, and stared hard.

My immediate reaction was to look away, but then I

forced myself to stare back. Why should I let him intimidate me?

'That must be them,' Gem whispered.

I knew it was, but didn't say so.

'They look okay,' Dad said. He smiled at Elaine and her son.

Gem waved at them.

I didn't smile or wave.

Nor did Elaine and her son. Elaine stared right through us, as if we were invisible and she was still waiting for someone else. Elaine's son bent his head to speak to her. She looked over at us, then nodded and turned and walked away.

'Oh! It couldn't have been them,' Gem said.

Elaine and her son disappeared around a corner.

Gem started laughing. 'They must have thought I was crazy waving at them – that's why they didn't wave back!'

'Lucky we didn't go up to them and demand they have an ice cream with us,' Dad said. 'We'd have been done for force feeding innocent people.'

Why had they turned and gone, just when we'd almost reached them?

We stood in the place outside the ice cream bar that Elaine and her son had vacated. I knew no other mother and son were going to arrive, but I didn't say so to Gem and Dad. I'd tried to tell Dad about the boys from Beechwood Academy picking on me once, I didn't want to have to do so again. Anyway, there was no point – I hadn't seen them for ages.

Dad and Gem were busy looking around, trying to be the first one to spot our date.

Ten minutes ticked by.

'They're a bit late,' Dad said.

Another five minutes ticked past.

'There they are!' Gem cried, pointing to a worn-out-looking woman, carrying four shopping bags and a rather cross-looking boy walking beside her.

'Come on, let's go and say hello,' Gem said, pressing a button on her electric chair.

I was about to say, 'Wait' but it was too late. Gem and Dad were already hurrying towards the woman and boy. I trailed after them. Could I be wrong?

Could these people be the real Elaine and her son? I didn't think so.

'Hi,' Gem said, stopping in front of them.

They stopped walking.

'Hello,' said the woman.

'Glad you could make it,' Dad said, smiling widely at them.

'Yes,' said Gem. 'We were starting to think you weren't going to turn up and Fifty Flavours is such a great place. I wasn't too bothered though, because Dad said we could have an ice cream anyway.'

I looked at the woman. She looked confused. The boy just looked grumpy.

'I'm sorry, I don't think I know you,' the woman said to Gem. She stared at the boy.

He shrugged. 'I don't know them.'

'They're not Elaine and her son,' I said.

The woman looked over at me. 'No, my name's Mary and this is my son, Jeff. We've been out shopping for some new clothes for him.'

'Come on, Mum,' Jeff said.

'Sorry,' said Dad. 'We thought you were someone else.'

'Why don't you come and have an ice cream, anyway,' Gem said. 'You look like you could do with one.'

'I could,' Mary agreed. 'Shopping with Jeff's hard work.'

'Mum!' Jeff said crossly.

'Why don't both of you come and have an ice cream with us,' Dad said.

'We'd better not,' said Mary. 'My husband's waiting for us at the car park. He can't stand shopping so he stays in the car. We should be getting back to him. He hates it if we're late. Thanks for the offer of an ice cream, though. I hope the people you're waiting for turn up.'

Mary and Jeff hurried away.

Dad looked at me and Gem. 'Looks like it's just the three of us,' he said. 'I don't think there's much point waiting any longer for Elaine and her son, do you?'

'No,' I said.

'But we are still going to have an ice cream?' Gem said.

'Of course,' said Dad. 'We deserve it.'

We went in to the Fifty Flavours Ice Cream Bar and ordered our favourites.

The ice creams made us forget about being stood up and we were soon laughing at the idea of trying to grab the unsuspecting Mary and Jeff and begging them to have an ice cream with us.

I was glad it was only the three of us. Relieved I hadn't had to sit anywhere near Elaine's son. He was probably just as pleased that he hadn't had to spend time with me.

I was positive it had been Elaine and her son standing outside Fifty Flavours when we first got there. But I still didn't say so to Gem or Dad.

'Two down and two to go,' I said to Gem. 'We haven't done very well so far.'

'Don't give up yet. There's still a 50% chance of catching someone in our mum trap,' Gem said.

'Yeah,' I agreed. I hoped the next two dates would be better than our first two. Advertising Dad hadn't got us the right results yet.

I saw Kate delivering letters down our street when I left the house for school on Monday morning. I ran over to her.

'Hi,' I said.

Kate grinned. 'Hi, how did the dates go?'

I'd told her about the dates we were going on when I'd seen her on Friday. I thought she had a right to know about them, because in a way she'd helped the dates to happen – or at least she'd delivered the packet of crucial letters to us.

'The second one didn't happen and the first one was a disaster,' I told her and went on to describe our date with the awful Janet and even more awful Olivia.

'No!' Kate said, when I told her Olivia had asked if I'd got peanut butter on my face. 'How rude.'

Rambo barked at us from Gummy's front garden as usual. I went over to stroke him, while Kate delivered a letter to the house next door.

'Morning, Mr Harris,' I called out, when I saw him standing in his porch. 'Have you found your false teeth yet?'

'No,' he said. 'But I'm not too worried. They've always found their way home before.' He grinned, showing his shiny pink gums.

Kate came to join me.

'Morning,' she said to Gummy and we carried on our way.

I told Kate about the avocado face mask and Leo coming round and saying he'd go to the disco with me. 'I was so embarrassed I had to keep a towel over my head when I was talking to him, so that he wouldn't see the green sick, avocado face mask I was wearing,' I said.

Then, because Kate hadn't had much of a chance to talk, but only to listen, I asked her, 'What did you do at the weekend, Kate?'

'Started my new fitness routine. Every day at 4.00 pm I'm going to jog through the park. I should be fit in no time.'

'But you must be fit already, all the walking you do delivering letters,' I said.

Kate shook her head. 'You haven't seen how much food I like to eat. I've got a *huge* appetite. No, a little jogging'll make sure I don't end up with a sparc tyre.'

I looked at my watch. I'd spent so long talking to Kate that if I didn't get a move on I'd be late for school.

'I have to go,' I said.

'Okay, 'bye.'

I hurried down the street and then came to an abrupt halt. In front of me were the boys from Beechwood Academy, the ones who'd picked on me. Lucky I was late, otherwise they'd have been behind me instead of in front.

Being trapped by them was my worst nightmare. Elaine's son was the meanest. He was the leader.

Luckily they didn't look behind them and see me. I ducked behind a postbox and waited until they were out of sight. They had one extra person with them today. Someone, who from the back and in the distance, looked like Olivia.

I remembered Janet's outrage that Olivia should be accused of bullying. If Olivia was hanging around with the Beechwood Academy boys, then maybe her last school hadn't been so wrong.

When I couldn't see them anymore I carried on to school. I knew I'd be late, but it was too bad. Late was better than bullied.

I hurried through the school gates and straight into class. Mrs Trent had just started taking the register.

I don't know how I'd expected Leo to react around me, now we were sort of seeing each other, or nearly seeing each other. I certainly hadn't expected him to carry on ignoring me – which is what he did.

Whenever I looked over at him he looked away, or suddenly became very interested in reading his computer magazine, or doing his homework, or just staring into space. But I knew he knew I was watching him.

Trying to speak to him was impossible. He just headed off in the opposite direction when he saw me approaching.

I hoped he wasn't wishing he hadn't asked me to the disco, because I still wanted to go with him – more than ever. Him acting as if he had second thoughts didn't make me like him any less. In fact, I think it made me like him more.

Why was he so strange? Why didn't he realise I was the girl of his dreams and treat me accordingly?

By breaktime I'd decided he must be expecting me to make the first move, but when I went to sit with him he moved away! I tried again at lunch but he jumped up as soon as I sat down, saying he wasn't feeling hungry anymore. He was behaving *very* strangely and *very* annoyingly. First, he said he'd go to the disco with me and now he was acting as if he couldn't stand being anywhere near me.

Leo didn't come back to class after lunch.

'Where is he?' I asked his best friend, Gary.

'Gone home,' Gary said. He doesn't like to waste words.

'Why?'

'Got chicken pox.'

'What!!'

Gary thought I hadn't heard him.

'Chicken pox.'

I went miserably back to my seat. The disco was only

two weeks away. Would Leo be able to go, or would he still have chicken pox by then? There was no one else I wanted to go with but him.

I wasn't sure what to do. Maybe chicken pox was the reason he had amnesia about asking me out. I knew I liked him, but did he really like me? Maybe he didn't know how he was supposed to act either. Should I buy a Get Well card and take it round to his house? That'd be the sort of thing a caring girlfriend would do. I just needed to find out exactly where he lived.

I went back to Gary.

'Leo lives over by the river, doesn't he?' I said.

'Nope.'

I waited a few seconds, but Gary must have thought he'd answered my question, because he didn't feel the need to say anymore.

'He always used to live there,' I prompted.

'Moved.'

Surprised, I asked, 'Where?'

'Um...Greenwood Gardens.'

'Greenwood Gardens!' I squeaked. It was the road that Gummy Harris lived in.

Gary opened his mouth, as if he was about to say something else, closed it, then opened it again. 'Number 33,' he said.

'33!'

Gummy Harris lived at number 29. I walked down Greenwood Gardens almost every day and hadn't once bumped into Leo. If I'd known he was living in number 33 I'd never have been able to walk naturally past it, or stop myself from staring through the windows.

Maybe it was just as well I hadn't known!

It'd be very easy to deliver a Get Well card to number 33. But maybe Leo'd rather I stayed away from him while his face was covered with spots. I hadn't wanted him to see my face when I'd had only one spot. I wished there was someone I could ask what to do.

After school I bought a Get Well card. I tried to think of something clever to write inside it. But couldn't think of anything, so finally I wrote, 'Hope you're feeling better soon and can come to the disco. See you Friday night, 7.30 at my place. Anna xxx.'

I turned into Greenwood Gardens but wasn't brave enough to ring Leo's doorbell or push the card through the letterbox.

Instead I ducked down behind his hedge and scuttled past, hoping he wouldn't be looking out and see me.

Rambo barked, and I hissed, 'Ssh!' as I ran past him and home.

Chapter 6

On Saturday we went to the Wild West theme park to meet Rodeo Sue.

Dad wore a blue jumper, so that no horses would mistake him for food. 'I'm more worried about meeting a hungry horse than meeting Sue,' he said.

'Do you think we should try to find Sue and say thank you for the tickets?' I said, when we got there. I was longing to see what she looked like. But Dad didn't think it was a good idea.

'She said she'd see us at the Cowhands Café after the show. She'll probably be busy getting ready for the show beforehand – we don't want to get in her way,' he said.

'Okay.'

'Let's have a look around,' said Gem.

'This place is massive,' said Dad.

There were loads of things to see and do. We had a go at shooting targets with air guns. We all scored a few hits, though none of us got the bull's eye target in the centre.

Gem had a go at archery and scored in the red. The Sioux supervising the archery was really impressed. Gem told him she belonged to an archery club at her school.

Then the three of us had a competition to see who was the best at throwing horseshoes over ten metal stakes, hammered into the ground. Dad won. To celebrate he bought us all double flavour ice creams. Then we went to explore the Wild West shop.

I liked the rings, necklaces and bracelets best, especially the ones with turquoise gem stones.

Dad tried on a cowboy hat. Gem tried a Native American headdress.

'Look, Dad, dream catchers!' I said.

'Dream catchers, what are they?' Dad said, taking off his cowboy hat and coming to look at a large circular dream catcher, made from feathers, leather and turquoise beads.

'You put it over your bed and it catches all the bad dreams and lets the good ones through,' Gem told him.

'I don't need a dream catcher,' Dad said. 'I never even remember dreaming. I just conk out as soon as my head touches the pillow and don't wake up until the alarm goes off the next morning.' He looked at the dream catcher price tag.

'They're very expensive.'

'These ones aren't,' I said, showing him some silver dream catcher pendants on leather thongs.

'Ooh, they're nice,' said Gem.

'Yes,' I said, holding one up to my neck. I looked at Dad. 'Can I have one?'

'I want one too, Dad,' Gem said. 'Please.'

Dad sighed. 'Go on, then.'

Gem and I each chose a dream catcher.

Dad paid for them. Then he looked at his watch. 'It's almost time for the show.'

Our seats were in the front row of the arena.

The Wild West show began with horses and riders cantering into the ring and racing round it. There was lots of shooting and hollering.

I grinned at Gem. 'This is excellent.'

'I wonder which one's Rodeo Sue?' Gem said.

There were four ladies amongst the show people. Any of them could have been Sue.

'Now tell me horses don't look scary,' Dad said, when one looked over the barrier at us and snorted.

Gem and I burst out laughing.

'No one's ever died of fright after being snorted at by a horse, Dad,' I told him.

Gem shivered dramatically. 'The terrible terror of ... the horse snort?'

'Ho, ho, ho, very funny,' said Dad.

'Cheer up, Dad,' I told him. 'If you put your hand up you might get picked to help with one of the acts. I bet the people sitting in these front seats always get chosen.'

Dad didn't look too pleased at the thought.

The Wild West crew raced out of the ring. Then it was time for the first act. Knife throwing.

A girl stood at one end of the ring and a cowboy, wearing a black leather costume, strode in and started throwing knives around – but luckily never in – the girl. It was pretty scary – one wrong move and she'd have been punctured.

'I hope they don't want volunteers for this,' I said. I

wouldn't like to have a lot of knives thrown at me. Fortunately the knife thrower didn't ask for anyone from the audience to help. After a few more knife-throwing tricks – including throwing some knives whilst blind-folded – the act was over.

'A big hand for Dan – our Knife Man,' said the ringmaster.

Everyone clapped and cheered loudly. I wondered if some of the audience were clapping because they felt relieved the knives hadn't been thrown at them. I know I was.

Dan, the Knife Man, and the girl who'd had the knives thrown at her took a bow.

Then four men, dressed as cowboys, pushed a mechanical rubber horse and two extra thick mats into the ring.

'Now, we want some volunteers from the audience to ride the Buckeroo – how about you, sir,' the ringmaster said, pointing straight at Dad.

Dad looked behind him, a bit like Leo did when I smiled at him, but it was obvious the ringmaster meant Dad.

'I don't think...' Dad started to say.

But the ringmaster didn't hear him.

'Come on, sir, it's perfectly safe,' he said into the microphone.

By now everyone in the audience was looking at Dad.

'Doesn't *look* safe,' Dad muttered.

But it was too late to back out. Two cowboys came over to Dad. One of them placed a cowboy hat on Dad's head. Reluctantly Dad went with them. They helped him to climb onto the Buckeroo horse.

'It has to be safe, doesn't it? They wouldn't let people from the audience do it, otherwise, would they?' I said to Gem.

Gem didn't reply. She was too busy watching Dad. He was sitting unsteadily astride the Buckeroo horse. He held the reins with one hand and the raised front of the saddle with the other.

'Poor Dad,' I said. 'I don't think he's going to like Buckeroo riding much.'

At first the Buckeroo horse rocked slowly back and forth. Dad looked slightly relieved. Then the horse started to go faster. Dad looked less happy. And faster. Dad looked scared. And faster still. Dad looked terrified. And the next second it was all over. Dad went flying off the Buckeroo horse and onto one of the mats.

'A big hand for our first Buckeroo rider,' the ringmaster said.

Dad struggled off the mats and gave his borrowed cowboy hat back to one of the cowboys.

I clapped and cheered Dad like crazy.

'Well done, Dad,' I said, when he returned to his seat, looking a bit shaky.

'Thanks,' he said. 'I'm glad it's over.'

'Was it really hard, Dad?' Gem asked him.

'Pretty hard,' Dad admitted.

The ringmaster asked for more volunteers and someone else was chosen to have a go on the Buckeroo.

The second man brought out of the audience to ride the Buckeroo lasted for even less time than Dad had.

And a third man's stay was shorter than Dad or the second man's.

'You were the best Buckeroo rider from the audience, Dad,' I told him.

Dad half smiled and said, 'I wouldn't want to do it again.'

'Let's see how a real rodeo rider rides,' the ringmaster said. 'Give a big hand for the best trick rider around – Rodeo Sue.'

I held my breath as Rodeo Sue came riding into the ring. Was she going to be our new mum? Would Dad like her? Would she like us? I hoped so.

Rodeo Sue had long curly red hair that bounced behind her as she rode. She circled the ring twice then took her feet out of the stirrups and the next second she was kneeling on the saddle instead of sitting on it, then standing up on the saddle, then standing on only one leg, with her hands out to the side for balance.

We all clapped her great riding. But Rodeo Sue wasn't finished yet.

She did a handstand on her horse and then circled beneath it and round the other side.

'She's great!' Gem cried, at the end of Sue's act.

All three of us clapped until out hands stung.

After the show we went round to the Cowhands Café to wait for Rodeo Sue.

She strode into the restaurant and over to our table about ten minutes later. Her face looked red. I supposed she must still be hot from doing her rodeo tricks.

'How-dee,' she said to us.

'Hi,' I said.

'You must be the best horse rider in the world!' said Gem.

'Hello,' said Dad.

'Do you arm wrestle?' Sue asked Dad. She flexed her impressive arm muscles. 'I can tell a lot about a man from how he arm wrestles.'

'Well . . . ' Dad said. We didn't do much arm wrestling at home.

'I know how to arm wrestle,' Gem said, putting her elbow on the table and holding up her fist.

Sue and Gem started to arm wrestle. Gem's arm went down fast.

'Let's do the best of three,' Sue said.

Sue won twice and Gem won the third time.

I was pretty sure Sue let Gem win. Should I ask Sue if she could French plait hair? What did she know about boys?

'How about you?' Sue said to me. 'Do you want to try arm wrestling?'

'Okay,' I said. I put my elbow on the table and my fist up. Sue's fingers grasped mine in a grip like a vice.

Sue let me win once out of three tries. She said the time I won I'd beaten her fair and square, which was kind of her, but not true.

'You're the best,' I said, and was about to ask her if she could French plait hair, when she turned to Dad.

'Your turn.'

Dad looked as if he'd rather not have a turn, thanks very much. But he didn't have much choice, if he didn't want to appear rude.

Reluctantly Dad put his elbow on the table and raised his arm. He was about to clasp Sue's hand when Knife Man Dan strode into the café and over to our table.

'How about trying that against me, instead of my woman,' Knife Man Dan said, sliding into the seat next to Rodeo Sue. He put an elbow on the table and stretched out his hand.

'I'm not your woman,' Sue said, folding her arms and looking cross. 'What are you doing here, Dan?'

Her face turned very red.

Knife Man Dan didn't listen to Sue.

'Come on,' he said to Dad. 'Let's see you wrestle.'

Dan's hand was much bigger, and a lot hairier, than Dad's.

'I don't think ... ' Dad started to say.

But Dan's hand enclosed Dad's. 'Best of three,' he growled.

Dad nodded.

It was all over in a few seconds. Dad's hand kept going down like a skittle. Dan didn't let Dad win any of the bouts.

When it was over Dad rubbed his wrist and flexed his fingers.

'You're such a brute, Dan,' Rodeo Sue said.

'I was only trying to protect you.'

'Well, I don't need protecting. Go back to the new girl you went off with – Tracey.'

'Today was Tracey's last show,' Dan said, turning to

look Sue in the eye. 'She's left the rodeo. Look I'm sorry, Sue, I should never have been taken in by her. You're the one I want, the only one I'll ever want.'

'Oh,' Sue said. Her face went even redder, she looked very happy.

I looked at Gem and shrugged.

The next second Sue and Dan had their arms around each other and were kissing.

I didn't want to watch them, but I made myself, because it might help when it came to me kissing Leo at the disco.

'Looks like Rodeo Sue's out of the running,' Gem whispered to me.

'Another one bites the dust,' I whispered back.

After a few minutes the three of us decided to leave Sue and Dan to it. As we were going out of the café I looked back. Sue and Dan were still wrapped around each other.

It was a shame Sue wasn't going to be our new mum, but she and Knife Man Dan did go together well, better than she could ever have done with our horse-fearing dad.

We only had one more lady from the newspaper left to meet.

'Please let Bibi be the one,' I wished and crossed my fingers.

Chapter 7

Bibi spotted us before we saw her.

'Coo-ee!' she shouted across the market square. She waved and then rushed towards us. 'Hello, it's so good to meet you all.'

'Hi,' I said.

'Hello,' said Gem.

'Hello,' said Dad.

Bibi took hold of Dad's arm. 'Shall we go in?'

'Er...yes,' said Dad.

Dad and Bibi had arranged for us all to have lunch at the 'King of Food' seafood restaurant.

'I think I'm going to like Bibi,' Gem whispered to me.

'Me too,' I whispered back. 'This could be the day we catch a mum in our mum trap, and decide not to throw her back.'

'Come on, you two,' said Dad.

We sat down at a table in the back of the restaurant and ordered some food.

Bibi didn't mind that Dad wasn't a fireman. She said she thought accountants could be just as sexy.

Dad said he'd never met a woman who thought accountants were sexy before.

Bibi looked pointedly at Dad and said she was only

referring to one particular accountant.

Bibi knew lots of good jokes, including some *really* rude ones, that Dad frowned a lot at.

It was easy to tell Bibi liked Dad. She sat as close to him on the bench seat as she possibly could – without sitting on his lap. Dad went all shy and kept moving away from her, but Bibi wasn't deterred, she just moved along as well. In the end Dad was blocked by the wall and had no choice but to let Bibi sit close to him or push her away.

I thought Dad would be pleased the advert had found him someone like Bibi. Someone who really, really liked him. But Dad didn't act pleased. He was very quiet, hardly smiled, didn't tell any jokes – although he knows loads – or even laugh at Bibi's ones. And he ate his lunch really fast. One second there was food on his plate and the next it had gone. If Gem or I had eaten our lunch as fast as him he'd have told us off for being so rude. But there he was gobbling his food down as if he was in an eating race.

'Well, that's that,' Dad said, as soon as he'd swallowed his last mouthful of pudding. 'I'll get the bill and then we'll have to be on our way. Hurry up, Gem.'

Gem had ordered a huge ice cream sundae for dessert. It was impossible to eat fast.

I could see Dad badly wanted to get out of the restaurant.

Maybe he feels sick, I thought, though if he did it was his own fault for eating so quickly.

I ate some of Gem's pudding for her.

What was Dad in such a rush for? He didn't look sick. Why did he eat all of his lunch and pudding if he felt sick?

And if he wasn't ill then why did we have to rush off, when we were having such a good time with Bibi? He hadn't mentioned anything urgent happening this afternoon. There couldn't be anything – he'd have told us.

'We must do this again sometime,' Bibi said, when Dad came back from paying the bill. She stroked Dad's arm.

Dad moved away so fast he almost fell over a passing waiter.

'Yes, let's,' Gem said enthusiastically.

I didn't say anything. Although I did want to meet Bibi again there was no point if Dad didn't want to meet her. Dad had to want the lady we caught in our mum trap as much as we did. Why was he behaving so strangely? I was very disappointed and more than a little bit cross with him. We'd finally found him someone who liked him and all he did was act as if Bibi had some contagious disease.

'I'll call you,' Dad said to Bibi. I knew he didn't mean it. Why was he lying?

'Make sure you do,' Bibi said, in her husky voice. She leant forward to kiss Dad, but he moved his face away and she kissed the air at the side of his face instead.

Outside the restaurant Bibi climbed into her red sports car.

'Ciao,' she said, and drove off with a roar.

'Phew! At last she's gone,' Dad said, when Bibi had disappeared round the corner. 'I've never met a more frightening woman.'

'Don't be such a wimp, Dad. She was good fun,' Gem laughed.

But I knew Dad was being serious.

'You didn't have her kneading your leg like it was a lump of dough,' Dad said. 'And if she'd sat any closer she'd have been on top of me.'

'But you are going to call her?' I said.

'I'm not,' Dad said.

'But, Dad . . . '

'No, no, no!' Dad said, waving his arms about to show he meant it. 'Never in a million years.'

When he was this definite about something it was just about impossible to get him to change his mind.

I sighed. 'Another one bites the dust,' I said.

'What did you say?' Dad said.

I looked at Gem. She shrugged.

'Nothing.'

Dad hurried us home, as if he couldn't wait to get back inside the bungalow and bolt the door.

'I've had enough of dates,' he said, later that afternoon. 'Thank goodness there's no one else to meet from the paper and this ordeal's finally over.'

I looked at Gem. She looked as miserable as I felt.

'But then we'll *never* have a new mum!' she cried.

'I can't help that,' Dad said, and he stomped out of the room.

'I don't think he'd be pleased if we advertised him again,' Gem said.

'No,' I said. 'It looks like our mum trap's failed. We'll never catch anyone now.'

'How're the dates going?' Kate asked me when I saw her a few mornings later.

'Not good,' I said, and told her about Rodeo Sue and Bibi. 'It all turned into a bit of a disaster. I don't see why Dad couldn't have liked Bibi – do you? She liked him lots and Gem and I liked her, why couldn't Dad have liked her too?'

'Morning,' Gummy Harris called, as we walked past his garden. Rambo was stretched out on the lawn, lazing in the morning sunshine.

'Morning.'

'What was it about Bibi your dad didn't like?' Kate asked.

I shrugged. 'I don't really know. He kept moaning about her sitting too close to him and touching his knee.'

Kate laughed. 'She does sound like a bit of a man-eater.'

'Maybe,' I agreed. I wished I'd paid more attention to Bibi – I'd always wondered what a man-eater was like.

'Never mind,' said Kate. 'I expect your dad's relieved it's all over. He did look a bit harassed when I saw him rushing off somewhere the other day.'

'Do you have a boyfriend, Kate?' I asked.

Kate shook her head. 'Free and single that's me.'

I looked at Kate. The questions I'd wanted to ask her about Leo flew out of my head. I had a much better idea. A brilliant idea!

Kate looked at my excited face. '*Oh no!*' she said. Then she burst out laughing. I like her laugh. It always makes me want to join in. When she'd finally stopped she said, 'Now, listen carefully, Anna. I haven't got a boyfriend and as far as I'm concerned I'm better off

71

without one – so don't you go getting any ideas about me and your dad.'

'Me? What ideas?' I said, trying to act innocent.

'You know,' Kate said.

I tried to look as if I didn't know what she was talking about. But Kate wasn't convinced. 'You know,' she repeated.

''Bye, Kate,' I said and went off to school, smiling to myself. I didn't know why I hadn't seen her as a potential candidate before. Kate could be just perfect, all I had to do was get her and Dad to see that. I was sure I'd be able to wear her down, given time.

But how was I going to mum trap Kate? How was I even going to get her into our bungalow? I had to find some way to force her to spend time with us. Once she really got to know us she was sure to like us.

I could try inviting her to dinner one evening, but that would look like a set-up and Kate was too wary for that kind of trick. And Dad might not like it much either.

What could Gem and I do that would look natural, but mean Kate had to come to our bungalow and stay there for a while? I couldn't think of anything.

I should have checked if Kate could French plait hair. I was pretty sure she'd be able to tell me all I needed to know about boys.

After school I had a meeting with Gem. At first Gem wasn't too sure about Kate.

'I haven't even met her,' she said. 'What if I don't like her?'

'You will like her,' I insisted. 'Anyone who met her

72

would like her.'

'Dad didn't. He said she couldn't take a joke.'

'That's because Dad didn't really get a chance to know her. He shouldn't have laughed at her, it was no wonder she got cross with him and stormed out. Look, I like her lots – you're bound to like her too.'

'Maybe,' Gem said, but she didn't sound too sure.

'Anyway,' I added, persuasively. 'If we don't try and get Dad to like her, there isn't anyone else to go in our mum trap. We've been through all the blind dates and Dad's never going to agree to put another advert in the paper. Think about it – do you really want a new mum or not – Kate could be our last chance.'

'I want one,' Gem said.

'Right,' I said. 'Help me think of a way to trap her. And remember this time the mum trap has *got* to work.'

'Why can't we just ask her round?'

'Because she's suspicious of my motives and she said she doesn't want a boyfriend. And Dad's had enough of dates, so he probably won't let us invite her, even if we could get her to come. If it feels forced they'll both be so on their guard there won't be a chance of anything romantic happening.'

'Hmm,' said Gem. 'This is going to be tough.'

'What we need is something that looks natural, but is really a set-up,' I said.

'Something sneaky?' said Gem.

'Yes, the sneakier the better. They might not like it at first, but if it works it'll all be worth it, and they'll thank us, in the end.'

'She hasn't met me, so she won't suspect I'm up to something – like she would you,' Gem said.

'No, that's right. You could be the bait that we use to reel her in. All we need to do is work out how to set our trap.'

'I wish I'd at least seen her,' Gem said.

I remembered Kate telling me about her daily jogging regime. 'I know – if you wait outside the park gates at 4 o'clock you might see her jogging past.'

'Okay,' Gem said. 'I'll try to work it so I see her, but she doesn't see me.' Gem thought for a moment and then added, 'Kate won't like it if she finds out what we're up to.'

I shook my head. 'Nor will Dad. So we'll just have to make sure neither of them suspects anything.'

'Let's sleep on it and see what ideas we come up with,' Gem said.

'Okay,' I agreed. I knew coming up with a mum trap that would work on Kate was going to be hard. Even *Girlfriend* didn't have any advice for this sort of situation. I'd been trying to think of a mum trap that'd work on Kate all day at school and hadn't thought of anything – although I'd been in trouble in two lessons for not paying enough attention.

Chapter 8

I was starting to panic, Leo was still not back at school and it was the disco on Friday. Would he be better by then?

I asked his friend, Gary, how he was.

'Back Wednesday or Thursday,' Gary told me.

I sighed with relief.

The Get Well card I'd bought for Leo was still in my bag. If I didn't give it to him today or tomorrow he'd be back at school and wouldn't even know I'd cared enough to buy him one.

I decided I had to be brave and after school I set off to deliver the card. So long as Leo didn't have a chicken pox relapse he should still be able to go to the disco with me.

But I was worried that everything would go okay. And *Girlfriend* hadn't been able to give me the sorts of details I needed. What would happen if Leo tried to kiss me? Were you supposed to close your eyes or keep them open? And did you close them when the kiss started, or when your faces were moving together? And if it was when your faces were moving together did your lips always meet, or did they sometimes miss and end up kissing each other's chins instead, or miss altogether and just kiss the air? It was all very confusing. And then, did you keep your lips closed or open? What about his brace – would that get in the way? Maybe he'd take it out before he kissed me but where would he put it – would he still be holding it when he put his arms around me – or would he put it in his pocket? But then it'd get all yucky when he put it back in his mouth and what if he wanted to kiss me again – he'd have to take it out again. I was glad I didn't have the problem of what to do with a brace too. It could get very awkward, even a little bit dangerous, if we both had braces.

I turned the corner into Greenwood Gardens.

'Hey, St John's scum!' someone shouted, and my heart stopped for a second and then started to thump hard.

I knew who it had to be. The boys from Beechwood Academy. I hadn't seen them for ages. Thought I was safe. What did they have to turn up now for?

Should I run away? They'd got longer legs than me, but fear would make me run fast. Maybe I'd be able to get away from them.

I looked behind me. There were the three who'd picked on me before and someone new – Olivia. Would she make them stop?

'Please help me, make them leave me alone,' I mind messaged to her. Would she understand? I looked at her face. She sneered at me. I wondered if I should tell her it made her face look very unattractive – but thought perhaps I shouldn't.

'Scared, are you?' Elaine's son said.

I shuddered. He might have become my step-brother if Dad and Elaine had met. He'd have made Gem and my lives hell.

'You should be,' said another of the boys.

Olivia just carried on sneering. I wanted to tell her to watch out because if the wind changed her face might get stuck like that. Fortunately, although fear was making my brain have crazy thoughts, I kept my mouth shut.

What would Olivia have been like as a step-sister? Too horrible to think about, she'd be just as bad as Elaine's son. I was glad our mum trap hadn't worked on either of their mums. Did they know both their mums wanted to meet my dad? I thought it better not to mention it.

By now the four of them were too close for me to run. I'd never get away. Should I scream? Shout for help? Would anyone hear?

'Give us your money, then,' Elaine's son said.

'Let's see what you've got in your bag,' another boy said and stretched out a hand.

I didn't want to give him my bag. I was really, really scared. But I didn't want him to have my bag with Leo's card inside it. Why wasn't there ever anyone around when I needed them?

And suddenly there was someone, or at least a great big *something*. A huge dog came racing towards me, barking ferociously.

'Here, Rambo, here!' I shouted.

The Beechwood Kids looked scared when they saw him.

'Let's get out of here,' one of the boys said. They ran off and Olivia went with them.

I knelt down and threw my arms around Rambo. I was almost crying with relief.

'You came just in time,' I said. 'Lucky they didn't know you don't have any teeth!'

Rambo licked my nose.

I looked over at Mr Harris. He was standing by the front gate he'd opened to send Rambo to my rescue.

'Come on, Rambo,' Mr Harris called.

Rambo bounded back to him.

'Thanks,' I said, walking over to him. 'I don't know what would have happened if Rambo hadn't come along.'

'Anytime, my dear,' Mr Harris said. 'I've seen those four going after other children too. You should report them. Can't let them go round intimidating people.'

I nodded. I was still a bit shaky. Tomorrow I'd tell the student counsellor at school what had happened. I didn't want anyone else to get picked on like I'd been.

I rang Leo's doorbell and a few seconds later he opened the door. The only sign that he'd recently had chicken pox was a scab on his nose. It made him look cute.

I smiled. He smiled back.

'This is for you,' I said, pulling the Get Well card out of my bag.

'I'll be back at school tomorrow,' he said.

'Good.'

There wasn't anything else to say. I went home.

'Have you seen Gem – she's not usually this late?' Dad said, when I got in. He kept staring out of the window, as if she'd magically appear if he looked often enough. 'Dinner's almost ready. She didn't say anything about going to an after-school club today, did she?'

I shook my head. If Gem had said she was going to be late, for any reason, Dad would have remembered. He always wants to know exactly where either of us is, who we're with, and when we'll get home.

'Maybe she's round at a friend's,' I suggested, although I already knew what Dad's reply would be.

'She'd have phoned,' he said, as I knew he would.

His anxiousness was starting to make me feel nervous. Gem was only half an hour late. She could have gone to the park to try and spot Kate, but that wouldn't have made her this late. Nothing could have happened to her, could it?

Another quarter of an hour went by. Dad was frantic.

'I'm going to phone round her friends and see if any of them know where she is,' he said.

As he picked up the receiver the doorbell rang.

Dad dropped the phone and ran to the door, I followed close behind.

On the doorstep stood Kate. She wasn't wearing her postwoman's uniform. She had on orange track-suit pants, a grubby white tee-shirt, a luminous green bandanna around her head, and her lucky skull and crossbone earrings in her ears. On her back was Gem, her arms clinging tightly around Kate's neck. Why was Kate giving my sister a piggyback?

Kate looked very hot and sweaty. Gem looked like she might have been crying. There were grey marks down her face which could have been wiped away tears.

'The battery on my chair went flat,' Gem said. 'I couldn't get it started again – I thought I was going to be stuck in that chair forever – no one even offered to help until Kate came jogging by.'

'But that battery's almost new – was it plugged in overnight?' Dad said.

'Excuse me, but . . . ' Kate said.

Gem shook her head. A tear rolled down her face. 'I forgot – I thought it'd be okay – would last long enough – but it didn't.' She sniffed.

I looked at Kate. Holding Gem must be exhausting.

'Come in, Kate,' I said, quickly. I pushed Dad to one side so she could get past.

Kate came in and deposited Gem on the sofa with a sigh of relief, then flopped down onto the sofa beside her.

'Where did your chair stop?' I asked Gem.

'Outside the park.'

Dad seemed to notice Kate for the first time. I didn't know if he recognised her as the postwoman, out of her uniform. 'Did you carry Gem back from there?' he asked.

Kate nodded. 'When the chair wouldn't move it seemed like the only thing to do. I was jogging to get fit – but walking – whilst carrying someone else is even better exercise!'

'No one's ever given me a piggyback that far before!' Gem said, and she started to laugh. 'Thanks, Kate.'

'Thank you,' Dad repeated after Gem. Then he remembered Gem's chair. It was too precious, as well as expensive, to leave out in the street. Even though someone would need to be a weightlifter to steal it, it still might get vandalised or damaged.

'Make Kate a cup of tea, Anna. I'll be back in a minute,' Dad said, checking the van keys were in his pocket. The van had been adapted to take Gem's chair in the back.

'Okay.' Gem's chair was great when it was working – but when the battery went flat the whole chair seized up. The wheels wouldn't go round and it was much much heavier than an ordinary wheelchair – more like trying to push a miniature car – with the hand brake on.

When Dad had gone, I said, 'I'll make that tea, unless you'd like something else, Kate. You can have anything you want. You deserve it.'

'Champagne, then?' Kate said. 'No, make that a big glass of ice cold Coke.'

'Make that two,' Gem said.

'Right.'

I came back a few minutes later with three Cokes and the biggest packet of crisps I could find.

'This should replace the calories I used up doing all that exercise,' Kate said, taking a large handful of crisps.

Dad came back a few minutes later.

'Get the chair, okay?' I asked.

'Yes,' Dad said. 'It didn't seem to have been touched.' He smiled at Kate. 'I can't thank you enough for bringing Gem back.'

'Why don't you ask Kate to stay to dinner?' Gem said, and then she winked at me. I couldn't believe it. Gem's wheelchair stopping and Kate's desperate rescue couldn't have been a deliberate mum trap – could it?

'Would you like to stay?' Dad said to Kate.

'I'd love to,' Kate said. 'Anyway, I'm too exhausted to move.'

'You just stay there then and I'll get busy,' Dad said. 'We're having spaghetti bolognaise.'

'My favourite,' said Kate and she took another large handful of crisps to keep her going until the dinner was ready.

'Kate,' I said.

'Yes?'

Now was my chance to ask her the question I was dying to ask.

'Can you do a French plait?'

'A French plait?' Kate said. 'I've never done one before, but it can't be that difficult, can it?'

'No-o,' I said. I didn't really know if French plaits were very difficult for another person to do on someone else, or not. I did know when I'd tried to do one on myself it had been very very difficult. In fact it could have been called a hair disaster. But maybe it was easier if you were doing it on someone else.

'Do you need one, then?' Kate said.

'Yes, urgently,' I replied. 'I want one for the school disco on Friday night.'

'I suppose I could have a go, if you like.'

'Would you – please.'

'Dinner's ready,' Dad called.

Dad tactfully didn't mention the Rambo incident throughout the evening. Nor did Kate. It was like they'd called a truce.

Dad was on his best behaviour and at his most charming. His garlic bread and spaghetti bolognaise were even more delicious than usual.

'Pop in anytime you fancy a cup of tea whilst doing your rounds,' Dad said, as we waved Kate goodbye, at the end of the evening.

When Kate had gone Dad started on the washing up. He was singing as he worked, so it was pretty safe for me and Gem to talk without being overheard.

'You didn't really pretend your electric was broken so we could mum trap Kate, did you?' I said.

''Course not!' said Gem. 'All I wanted to do was see what Kate looked like. After school I waited by the park gate for her to go jogging past at four o'clock, like you told me she did.

'I spotted her almost immediately, because she was wearing those skull and crossbone earrings of hers. I smiled at her and she smiled back and went running into the park. When she was out of sight I switched on my chair, ready to rush back here and tell you I thought Kate would be a great lady to catch in our mum trap.

'But when I tried to get my chair moving nothing happened. The battery was dead. No one would help me until Kate came running back out of the park. I really, really like her, Anna.'

'Me, too,' I said.

'Some enchanted evening!' Dad's voice sang from the kitchen.

'I think Dad likes her too,' we laughed.

Chapter 9

Kate was waiting for me at the bungalow, when I got home from school on Friday, the disco night.

It was time to see if she could fulfil the first requirement of the ideal mum – to be able to French plait hair.

'Hi, Kate, thanks for coming,' I said.

'That's okay. I know how important it is that you look good for the disco. Shall I have a practice at doing a French plait on you before you have your shower?'

I looked at my watch. Three and a half hours before Leo would be round. I could devote half an hour to letting Kate practise her French plaiting on me. After all, I wanted it to be perfect.

We went into my bedroom and I sat on a chair and Kate set to work. First she brushed my hair, then she said, 'I think it'd be best to start quite high on your head. French plaiting is a bit like weaving, you take one strand from one side and one strand from the other and weave them around the strand in the middle.'

As she talked she took strands of my hair between her fingers.

She sounded and looked like she knew what she was doing. I decided it was time to find out how she would do on my second mum requirement.

84

Having someone like Kate to answer questions was even better than *Girlfriend* magazine, because I could ask Kate the questions I really wanted to know the answers to.

'Kate?'

'Yes?'

'What can you tell me about boys?'

'Boys,' Kate frowned. 'Boys are very confusing and when they grow up they turn into men, who are even more confusing.'

I knew that already. Maybe I needed to be more specific.

'How about kissing boys?'

'Hmm,' Kate said. 'Kissing. Well...'

'Yes?'

'Okay. Don't eat raw onions before you kiss someone, unless he's been eating raw onions too. The same goes for garlic.'

'Right,' I said. 'Anything else?'

'Um...this French plaiting is a lot harder than it looks,' Kate said. She twisted a hair band into the bottom of the plait, then stood back.

'There, you're done.'

I stared into the mirror. Kate's French plaiting looked fine from the front. I turned my head to the side. My hairstyle didn't feel very secure. A large section of hair slipped out of the plait.

I turned my head the other way and more hair fell out of the plait. I looked a mess.

'Needs to be tighter,' Kate said. She unplaited my hair

and set to work again. 'The worst kissing horror experience I ever heard of was when a friend of mine, called Keli, kissed her first boyfriend and he fainted. Not a very good start to a kissing career.'

'No,' I said. I hoped Leo wouldn't faint if I kissed him.

'There,' Kate said. 'Finished.'

I looked at myself in the mirror. Kate had made this French plait a lot tighter. Very tight.

'What do you think?' Kate asked, when I didn't say anything.

I had a French plait. Something I'd wanted for ages. Something that was supposed to make me look sophisticated like Jenny Carter. But it didn't make me look sophisticated. It made me look awful.

'Anna?'

My head looked really small. My face looked pinched.

I pulled out the hair band.

'Thanks for trying, Kate,' I said. 'But I think I like my hair down better.'

'Good choice,' Kate said. 'You'll feel much more comfortable with a style you're used to. Take it from me, drastic hairstyle changes before a big date aren't usually a good idea.

'Anyway, good luck for tonight. Just be yourself and you'll be fine. I'm covering for someone at the sorting office, so I need to get back there.'

'Okay,' I said. 'Thanks, Kate.'

'Anytime.'

''Bye.'

When Kate had gone I looked at my watch. Leo would be at the bungalow in three hours. I needed to get ready.

'Anna,' Gem said, coming into my room.

'Yes?'

'You can borrow this if you like,' Gem said, holding out her best bracelet.

'Thanks.'

'And,' she added, her voice lowering to a conspiratorial whisper.

'Yes?'

'I saw Dad kiss Kate.'

'Did you!'

'It was just a little kiss,' Gem admitted. 'But still.'

'Yes,' I agreed. This was very good news indeed. But there was no time to talk about it now. I had to get ready. I hurried into the bathroom.

'Anna, I need to use the loo sometime this evening,' Dad groaned, an hour later.

'Okay, okay,' I said.

'And do you need to use so much hot water? The bill's going to be enormous!' he moaned.

How could he be worrying about money at a time like this? I decided to ignore him. It wasn't his fault. Only another woman would understand.

At 7.30 precisely the doorbell rang.

'Get that, will you, Dad,' I called.

'Why can't you get it?' Dad called back.

I sighed. 'Because I need to check I look okay, of course.'

'But you've been getting ready all evening.'

'Just do it, Dad, please,' I said and disappeared into my bedroom to make sure my clothes really did look okay from the front, back and sides. My hair was going to stay just the way I wanted it to, my skin hadn't given birth to a spot, and my teeth didn't have any stray bits of food lurking in them.

'Leo's here,' Dad called. I came out of my bedroom.

Leo was sitting on the very edge of the sofa, looking uncomfortable. Dad and Gem were staring at him with all the enthusiasm of scientists who'd discovered a previously unknown specimen.

I put Leo out of his misery.

'Come on,' I said. 'Let's go.' I kissed Dad. 'See you later, Gem.'

'Have a good time,' Gem said.

'Don't be too late,' said Dad.

I was very glad Leo was healthy enough to go to the disco with me.

'I'm glad your chicken pox went,' I said to him, as we walked back to school.

'Me, too,' said Leo. 'I've never wanted to scratch so much in my life.'

The deputy head was collecting entrance fees from the discogoers.

Leo and I each paid for ourselves and went inside. The hall looked very different with the gym equipment gone. It felt different too, less schoolish, more exciting. The music was really loud and coloured lights cast different coloured shadows around the walls.

'Let's dance,' I said, and pulled Leo towards the centre of the hall.

Leo's dancing consisted of side to side swaying, with stiff legs and arms held rigidly at his sides. He looked a bit like a robot. I'd never really thought about how Leo would dance before. He looked almost as uncomfortable and self-conscious as when Dad and Gem had been staring at him.

'Loosen up, Leo,' I told him, 'this is supposed to be fun.'

He nodded and tried to smile, but it came out as a grimace.

Which made it all the more surprising when three dances later he'd really, really loosened up, and I started to wonder whether I should tell him to go back to dancing like a robot.

Leo, I'm sure, thought he looked great. It wasn't his fault that other people didn't appreciate the uniqueness of his movements.

As Leo became caught up in the music he danced like someone stepping on hot coals, with ants in his pants, whilst swotting a swarm of wasps hovering around his head. His hair got soaked and sweat trickled down his face, flicking spray outwards.

I took Leo's arm. 'Let's sit down,' I said.

Leo sat for a few minutes and then wandered off to the loo. I waited for five minutes, then spotted him talking with the computer teacher, so I went to dance with some of the other girls and had a great time because, although I thought I might be in love with Leo, it was much more fun dancing with the girls.

Towards the end of the evening the DJ started to play some slow dances. I went to sit down.

'I hate slow dances,' one of the girls said.

Leo came over. He took my hand. I stood up.

Leo might have been too unusual for me in the fast dances but I wouldn't have swopped him for anyone else in the world when it came to slow dancing.

The slow robot movement with his arms wrapped around me and my face next to his felt just right.

Much too soon the music stopped and the lights were switched on. It was time to go home.

The evening had flashed by.

Quarter of the way home Leo put his arm around me.

Half way home we stopped to kiss, but didn't quite make it to each other's lips because our noses got in the way. My nose got a bit squashed.

Three quarters of the way home Leo tripped up.

'Are you okay?' I cried, kneeling beside him to check he wasn't hurt.

'Yes, I'm okay,' he said. He picked up a lump of earth. 'There's something sharp in this,' he said, and started to brush the soil away. A minute later he was holding a very old, not very white, pair of false teeth.

There couldn't be that many people missing false teeth.

'They're Gummy Harris's!' I said.

'He won't be gummy once he's wearing these,' said Leo.

'I hope he gives them a really good wash before he puts them back in his mouth.'

We walked over to Gummy Harris's house and rang the

doorbell. Rambo started barking like crazy.

'His bark's worse than his bite,' I said.

Mr Harris opened the door a fraction, but sensibly kept the chain on.

'Yes?' he said suspiciously.

'It's me, Mr Harris,' I said, 'Anna, and this is my er – boyfriend, Leo. You know him, he lives two doors along from you. We've brought you a present.'

'A present?'

Leo pushed the false teeth through the door crack.

'Well, I never,' said Gummy Harris. He unhooked the chain. 'My missing false teeth. Where did you find them?'

'They found us,' I said. 'Leo tripped over them.'

'Now you'll be able to chew raw carrots again, if you want to,' Leo said.

'Oh, I can't wear them,' Gummy said, 'not in front of Rambo. He'd be jealous if I had false teeth and he didn't. Though I suppose I could always put them in for a little while when he's out. Thanks very much for bringing them back to me.'

''Night, Mr Harris,' we said.

Leo and I carried on walking home. I told him how Rambo and Mr Harris had helped me when the kids from Beechwood Academy had tried to take my bag.

By the time I'd finished we'd reached the bungalow.

Leo bent his head to kiss me and this time I kept my face still and just waited for his lips to find mine. It was magic. I felt all melty inside. This had to be love!

''Bye, Anna,' Leo said. 'See you at school on Monday.'

''Bye.'

After a few steps he turned and called out: 'Do you want to go to the pictures tomorrow?'

I nodded and grinned so wide I thought my face would crack. 'Yes.'

'Pick you up about seven?'

'Right.'

''Bye.'

''Bye.'

I took my key out of my pocket and let myself in. I was bursting to tell someone how my date had gone.

Dad was fast asleep on the sofa in front of the TV. Gem was curled up beside him, fast asleep too. It seemed mean to wake them up.

I sighed and headed towards the kitchen to get myself a drink.

Then I saw Kate, sitting at the kitchen table.

'Hello,' I whispered, so as not to wake Dad, or Gem. 'I thought you'd gone to the sorting office.'

Kate shook her head, smiled and whispered, 'I came back.'

'What are you doing in here?'

'Waiting for you,' Kate said. She stood up, opened the freezer and pulled out a big tub of ice cream. Then she took two spoons from the drawer and sat down.

She kept a spoon for herself and gave one to me, before opening the ice cream.

'Go on,' she said. 'I want to hear all about it.'

I grinned and dug my spoon deep into the ice cream. I was very glad the mum trap had brought Kate into our lives.